Born in Edinburgh, ... years living in Scotland, followed by five years ... eighteen years in London before returning to Scotland in 1993.

Her school ... Edinburgh.

Carole's working career started with two years in the Bank of Scotland followed by a very exciting life working for two airlines and as a travel agent which enabled her to fulfil a lifetime of travelling to many wonderful and exotic parts of the world.

Moving to Aberfoyle, Perthshire, in 1993 for two years, she then spent more than ten years living in the beautiful village of Balmaha, on East Loch Lomond.

*

The idea for the books came from her granddaughter Sophie, who asked her to read one of her schoolbooks.

At the end of the reading, Carole thought 'I can write better than this.'

As co-owner of the village shop with her late husband, she sold a variety of adorable Scottish teddy bears, each dressed in tartan tammies, scarves and 'Balmaha Bear' embroidered sweaters.

All the characters for the books are named after local residents of Balmaha and their occupations although she stopped short of saying whether she would go as far as to base the character's personalities around people she knew.

A selection of fourteen bears were chosen as characters, each with a separate family or clan name:

Mrs Anderson Bear – Schoolteacher
Buchanan Bear – Builder
Mrs Campbell Bear – Storekeeper
Forbes Bear – Fisherman
Fraser Bear – Innkeeper
Miss Graham Bear – Doctor
Hamilton Bear – Beekeeper
Murray bear – Farmer
Mrs MacDonald Bear – Weaver
MacFarlane Bear – Boatbuilder
MacKay Bear – Carpenter
MacKenzie Bear – Tailor
Miss MacLean Bear Nurse
MacMillan Bear – Plumber
Not forgetting Baby MacDonald Bear – The mischievous one!

The Bears adventures were inspired by the beautiful surroundings of Balmaha and Loch Lomond.

Carole now lives in Hawick in the Scottish Borders with her new husband of six years, who is also an author.

The Balmaha Bears

The Legend

Carole Meara

The Balmaha Bears
The Legend

Olympia Publishers

London

www.olympiapublishers.com
OLYMPIA PAPERBACK EDITION

A CIP catalogue record for this title is
available from the British Library.

ISBN: 978-1-84897-444-9

(Olympia Publishers is part of Ashwell Publishing Ltd)

First Published 2003 (Glowworm Books Ltd.)
First Revision Published 2010 (Balmaha Bears Books)

Some of the grammar in this book is expressed in the Scottish idiom

This Edition Published in 2014

Olympia Publishers
60 Cannon Street
London
EC4N 6NP

Printed in Great Britain

For my grandchildren;
Jamie & Sophie Clarke
Elle, Cameron & Harris McMillan

The Balmaha Bears loved stories. The children's favourite was 'The Legend', the story of the Balmaha Bears and how they came to live in their big underground cave. The best storyteller was Fraser Bear the Innkeeper, the oldest and wisest bear.

"Long, long ago, our ancestors were huge brown bears who lived in caves around Loch Lomond.

They ate sweet berries in autumn and ripe fruits in summer, they caught fat fish in the loch and collected sticky honey from the bees. All bears love honey, don't they?"

The little bears rubbed their tummies and licked their lips.

"One year the weather was terrible and every year after that it became worse. The lochs, rivers and streams froze over and deep snow covered the bears' favourite bushes. They couldn't find enough food and their stores of nuts and berries were running very low. How would they survive?"

"But things were even worse than that. Human beings who lived nearby were cold and hungry too, and some of them hunted the bears so that they could keep themselves warm with their thick, warm, furry coats."

The little bears gasped in horror and clung tightly to each other. "I don't want to lose my warm, furry coat," cried Mrs Fraser Bear.

"The bears who escaped hid in caves near here at Balmaha. As the years went by, they went deeper and deeper under the mountains, living quietly and safely on roots, mosses, and small herbs that they found. The cave roofs got lower and lower and over time, the bears became smaller and smaller, until they were the size we are now."

"But how did they find this special cave?" asked Baby MacDonald Bear.

"Miss Graham Bear the Doctor, found it when she was looking for berries. When she told the others about this magical place, with running water, buzzing bees, and singing birds, they couldn't wait to see it."

"Buchanan Bear the Builder, said it was just the place to build houses and he asked MacKay Bear the Carpenter, to help. Before long, they had all moved into their new homes. There were trees, berry bushes, lots of plants nearby, and a stream with trout and salmon. Some of the bears found little tufts of wool and made soft beds for everyone. They'd been dropped by the birds who nested in the roof of our cave. It was perfect!"

13

"But where did the light come from, Fraser Bear?" asked a little voice.

"Light came from the same white quartz Daylight Stone we know today. We still don't know how, but it seems to trap sunshine from those little gaps in the roof, the spaces the birds and bees use to fly in and out. Then the Daylight Stone shines for all it's worth. What would we do without it?"

The little bears sighed; they couldn't imagine living in the darkness.

"But what did they do next?" they asked.

14

Fraser Bear laughed. "There was lots to do. Murray Bear the Farmer, planted seeds so they could have flour. Hamilton Bear collected honey and Mrs Hamilton Bear made honey cakes. Fraser Bear made their favourite drink, Heather Honey Nectar, and Forbes Bear was best at fishing. The young Balmaha Bears went to Mrs Anderson's Bear's school each morning and helped to gather nuts and berries in the afternoon for Mrs Campbell Bear's store cupboard."

"Where did our clothes come from?"
asked another small bear.

"That was Mrs MacDonald Bear's idea. Some of the older bears couldn't always tell who was who, so she designed special tartans for each family. She used berry juices, mosses, and crushed brightly coloured pebbles to make the colours and dyed lots of wool. Then MacKay Bear made a loom and they wove the cloth. MacKenzie Bear the Tailor, made the scarves, tammies, and kilts."

"That's why we all have different tartans. We're all Balmaha Bears, but we're all just a wee bit different."

Fraser Bear always ended his story like that.
The young bears clapped their paws and
growled happily. They'd heard it again and
again and they loved it every time.

"Now here are your mums and dads to
take you home for tea. Off you go!"

One little bear was missing. Mrs MacDonald
Bear was frantic.

"Baby MacDonald Bear must have
wandered off on his own," said the others.
"He was definitely here at the start."

The search was on.

"I've found his tammy!" yelled MacFarlane Bear the Boatbuilder, and all the bears rushed towards him.

"Quiet!" he ordered. "I'm sure I can hear something." Silence fell and sure enough they could hear faint baby-bear squeals coming from beyond the cave wall.

"How did he get in there?" asked a very surprised MacKay Bear. "There must be an opening somewhere."

They searched frantically. At last Buchanan Bear shouted, "Here's an opening but it's far too small for any of us to get through."

18

"Let's get digging and hurry up," said Fraser Bear, and the bears set to work.

They dug, and dug and the young bears hauled the stones away from the hole. The cries were getting louder as the hole got bigger and bigger.

"Let me try and get through," said Miss MacLean Bear. "I'm the skinniest bear!"

She poked her head
through and said, "Yes, that's
him! I can see his scarf! I'll
wriggle through and fetch him."

Bears have rather large bottoms so Buchanan Bear
had to squeeze and push and shove until they heard her
shout, "Got you, you rascal!" Then there was
a long silence before she shouted, "Come quickly!
You won't believe what we have found!"